This book belongs to:

_____

_____

www.winslowpress.com

My Building

WINSLOW PRESS

For Riley
R.I.A.

To my son, Dan
I.B.

My Building

Robin Isabel Ahrens

Illustrations by Ilja Bereznickas

The apartment building where I live
Has twenty-seven floors.
All kinds of people come and go
Through hallways lined with doors.

Behind each door there is a home,
And no two look the same.
I catch a glimpse of furniture
Or a picture in its frame.

I notice other pleasant things
When passing by each door,
Like music from the stereos
And cooking smells galore.

On weekdays I see daddies
    And some mommies in their suits,
A policeman who's off duty
    And a man in cowboy boots!

I wave to all the children
Who leave for school at eight,
And older kids in fancy shorts
Who bike or roller skate.

I like the white-haired couples,
Who smile each time we meet.
They put on special hats and coats
To walk along the street.

I find help for the nannies
   Whose strollers can't get through.
My favorite has a set of twins
   Dressed up in pink and blue.

I pet the dogs both tall and small
Who exercise each day.

They bark and strain their leashes
As they rush outside to play.

Deliverymen march through the halls,
With things that look so grand,
Like flowers wrapped in cellophane
Or food from every land.

They all chat with the super,
 Whose keys go *clink-clink-clink*!
He brings a big red toolbox
 When he comes to fix our sink.

The mailman nods and winks at me
When he stops by at ten.
He fills the boxes one by one,
Then locks them up again.

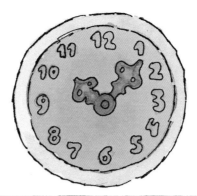

I salute the smiling doorman
In his uniform so neat.
He wishes me, "Good day! Have fun!"
And leads me to the street.

From there I see my building,
    Which almost scrapes the sky.
I'm glad to be a part of it—
    Not just a passerby.